IN SEARCH OF THE SAVEOPOTOMAS

written by: Stephen Cosgrove
illustrated by: Robin James

A Serendipity Book

Printed in U.S.A.

ISBN #0-915396-00-9 IN SEARCH OF THE SAVEOPOTOMAS

Dedicated to:
Winifred Russe,
the original Saveopotomas.

Millions and millions of years ago, before there were animals as we know them today, the world was inhabited by dinosaurs. They would run and play and just have fun, day in and day out.

Out of all the creatures in the world at this time, there was one who had no fun whatsoever...the Hoardasaurus.

He would constantly be looking this way and that, mumbling to himself, "Oh dear! What shall I do? Oh dear!"

For you see, that poor Hoardasaurus had spent his entire life hoarding all the things that were valuable to him. He had hoarded an old bone, a broken chain, a piece of rock, a yo-yo with no string, and of course, silver.

That poor Hoardasaurus was always looking over his shoulder, wondering and worrying! He was so afraid that someone would try to steal all the valuables he had hoarded over the years.

The Hoardasaurus had one friend out of all the animals of the kingdom, a small, fluffy bird called a Glink.

The Glink, on occasion, had been known to ride on his friend's head; but lately that was almost impossible. The Hoardasaurus was turning and running so fast that the Glink could not hold on. Half of the time he would be knocked off by a branch as they went zipping and pacing by.

One day the Glink could take it no longer and finally shouted, "STOP!"

Well, believe you me, that Hoardasaurus did stop! For a Glink had one of the loudest voices in the kingdom.

"Hoardasaurus," said the Glink, "why do you pace so much?"

"Because," stuttered the Hoardasaurus, "if I stop moving, someone will steal all that I have hoarded. Then I won't have anything and I'll have to start all over again!"

The Glink began to think, while the Hoard-asaurus nervously peeked over his shoulder and dashed to look behind a bush.

"I have it!" shouted the Glink. "We shall search out the Saveopotomas. He, out of all the creatures, knows how to save and will solve your problem."

The Hoardasaurus thought for just a moment, looked between his legs to see if anyone was behind him, and agreed.

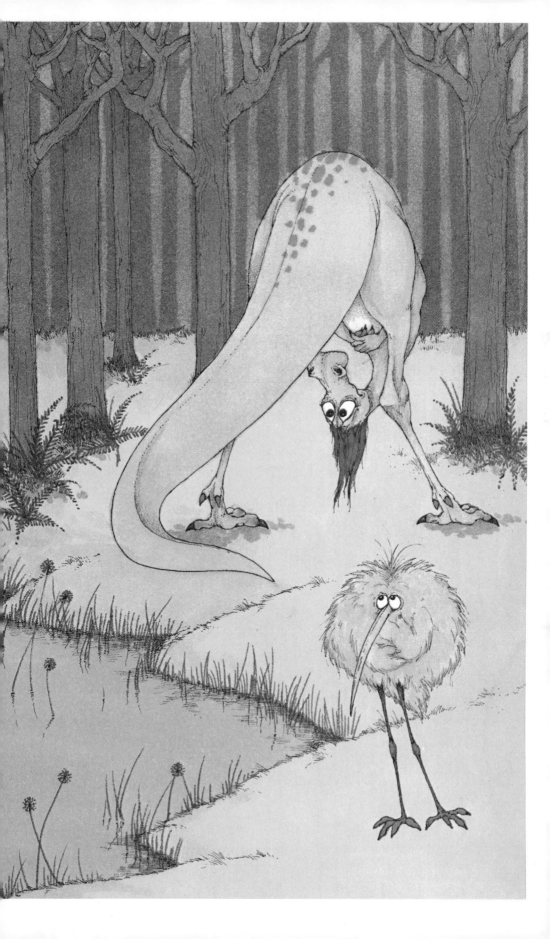

So the two of them picked a very large banana leaf, laid it on the ground, and, oh so very carefully, began placing all of the valuables in it.

They packed the yo-yo with no string, the piece of rock, and, of course, all of the silver. Then they rolled up the leaf, tied it with a piece of vine; and set off in search of the Saveopotomas.

They walked and ran as fast as they could, searching and asking for the Saveopotomas.

"Have you seen him?" they asked a large brontosaurus sitting in the middle of a lake.

The brontosaurus stopped and thought for a moment while chewing on a big chunk of grass. "Hmmmm," he rumbled. "As I remember, he lives just on the other side of that mountain there."

With that, he sank with a bubble and a burp to the bottom of the lake.

The Hoardasaurus and the Glink hurried nervously on their way, looking this way and that. Finally they arrived at the base of the mountain and stopped.

The Hoardasaurus looked up and saw how high he must climb. "Oh no!" he cried. "I'll never make it across the top with all of my valuables, and if I leave them here, someone will surely steal them!"

With that, he sat down with a plop on his bag and began to cry large dinosaur tears. The Glink thought for a moment and said, "You have hoarded all your life to gather your riches and now have more than you could ever use in two lifetimes." The Hoardasaurus reluctantly agreed.

"Why don't you give away what you don't need or want, so that no one will steal it? What is left, you can easily carry to the Saveopotomas."

The Hoardasaurus sat there for a while and then agreed, because it seemed to be the only solution.

The Glink quickly gathered all the animals and dinosaurs together. One by one the Hoardasaurus gave away all that he had hoarded these many years.

He gave away pieces of silver, his favorite broken rock, and the yo-yo with no string. You know, the more the Hoardasaurus gave away, the less nervous he felt. When the last animal had received his share, the Hoardasaurus felt pretty good all over.

With enough silver left to last him the rest of his life and his favorite old bone, the Hoardasaurus and his friend, the Glink, easily climbed the mountain and reached the land of the Saveopotomas.

Once there, they asked the Saveopotomas to save the rest of the silver for them until such time as they should need it.

The Saveopotomas dutifully entered the total amount of silver on a large leaf and gave a copy to the Hoardasaurus.

"What about the bone?" asked the Saveopotomas.

"I shall keep it as a reminder never to hoard again!" said the Hoardasaurus.

So the two of them set off for their home, with the Hoardasaurus peeking, just once in a while, over his shoulder, because he was just a little nervous about his favorite old bone.

So if you take up hoarding
And are thinking only of you,
Remember the Hoardasaurus
...And the Saveopotomas too.